Lucy
the Flying Cat

Written by
Maralyn Calton
Illustrated by **Bailey Garza**

**For Lucas and Sofia,
our littlest siblings**

Lucas
the Flying Cat

Hi, I am Lucas.

I am a cat that can fly.

I can fly fast.

I can fly high.

I can fly low.

I can fly to school.

I can fly to the park.

tweet
tweet
tweet
tweet

The End

Maralyn Calton is a playwright, and has been writing and directing children's plays since she was 13. Having a daughter made her realize she could do so much more for kids and she started writing children's books. Maralyn lives in a small coastal town in Texas with her daughter and husband, where they enjoy their daily visits to the beach and their plethora of books.

Bailey Garza is an awarding-winning artist. She loves to create anything from sketches to beautiful landscapes. She was ecstatic about the opportunity to illustrate and couldn't wait to get started. When Bailey's not busy doing art she's usually chasing her two kitties around, or having adventures with her husband in the beautiful mountains of Utah.

Find activities and coloring pages to print at home, and learn more about upcoming Magic Animals books at www.AndPubCo.com/magic

CPSIA information can be obtained
at www.ICGtesting.com
Printed in the USA
LVHW070848170522
718964LV00007B/64